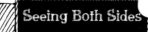

Seeing Both Sides

Summer School, Yes or No

Erin Palmer

MW00995140

Rourke
Educational Media

rourkeeducationalmedia.com

Scan for Related Titles
and Teacher Resources

Before Reading:

Building Academic Vocabulary and Background Knowledge

Before reading a book, it is important to tap into what your child or students already know about the topic. This will help them develop their vocabulary, increase their reading comprehension, and make connections across the curriculum.

1. *Look at the cover of the book. What will this book be about?*
2. *What do you already know about the topic?*
3. *Let's study the Table of Contents. What will you learn about in the book's chapters?*
4. *What would you like to learn about this topic? Do you think you might learn about it from this book? Why or why not?*
5. *Use a reading journal to write about your knowledge of this topic. Record what you already know about the topic and what you hope to learn about the topic.*
6. *Read the book.*
7. *In your reading journal, record what you learned about the topic and your response to the book.*
8. *After reading the book complete the activities below.*

Content Area Vocabulary
Read the list. What do these words mean?

condensed
continuity
crucial
distraction
examine
extracurricular
humiliating
mastered
obligations
persuade

After Reading:

Comprehension and Extension Activity

After reading the book, work on the following questions with your child or students in order to check their level of reading comprehension and content mastery.

1. *What is an opinion? (Summarize)*
2. *How do personal experiences shape someone's opinion? (Infer)*
3. *What are some other ways not listed in the book that summer school benefits students? (Asking questions)*
4. *What are some reasons you might want to attend summer school? (Text to self connection)*
5. *What could happen if schools were not allowed to offer summer school classes? (Asking questions)*

Extension Activity

Share your thoughts! Create a brochure that highlights your opinions about summer school. Ask classmates to tell you their opinions. Use their input to add to your own ideas about the topic.

Table of Contents

Taking Sides

Summer vacation is something most students look forward to all year long. But not all students get the summer off. Some students spend part of their summer in the classroom. What do you think about summer school? Are you for it or against it?

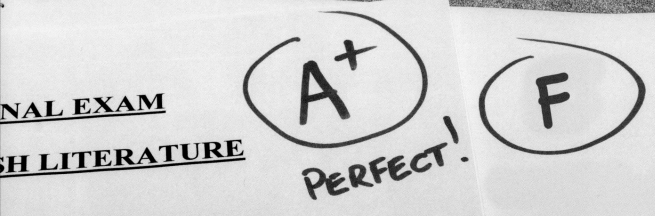

NAL EXAM

SH LITERATURE

A+ PERFECT! **F**

#1 AND ANSWER THE FOLLOWING:

eight of 8"

tagonist.

tic fallacy and show one example from the text.

is trying to convey.

#2 AND ANSWER THE FOLLOWING:

Facts, research, and personal experience are some things that can shape your opinion.

Before you make a decision about whether you agree or disagree with something, it's a good idea to **examine** both sides of the issue.

Let's consider the points of view of those for and against summer school. Then you can decide which side you are on.

Summer School? Yes, Please!

Some students work hard throughout the year, but haven't **mastered** the material required to advance to the next grade level. It is important to give these students another option before making them repeat an entire grade.

Students may not pass every subject the first time. Many students need more individual attention. It can be difficult for teachers to have enough one-on-one time for each student in a large class.

Reality ✓

Some students are required to attend summer school to make up credits they need to move on to the next grade. But others choose to go to summer school to get ahead or learn something new.

Summer school programs often have less students, so those who struggled during the year can get the focused attention they need to learn the material that they had a hard time with before.

Without the option of summer school, students that just need a little extra help can end up falling an entire year behind.

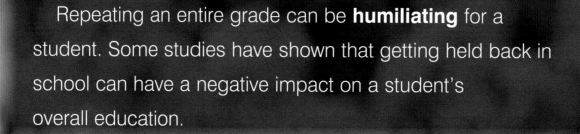

Repeating an entire grade can be **humiliating** for a student. Some studies have shown that getting held back in school can have a negative impact on a student's overall education.

Reality ✓

Research shows that students who had to repeat a grade in elementary school were less likely to graduate high school.

There are other reasons why students may attend summer school. Some schools offer summer options to keep students learning and help them get ahead.

Subjects, like math, often build upon previous lessons each day. **Continuity** is important. This means that taking months off from learning can make it much harder to learn.

Summer school can help keep everything you learned before in your head so you can move forward without taking any steps back.

Summer school is also a chance to study subjects you didn't have time to learn during the school year. Some schools offer summer options in subjects that don't fit into the regular school year.

Summer school is usually shorter than a traditional school day, which leaves plenty of time for summer fun. Since teachers know that students are not usually very excited to attend summer school, they usually incorporate fun activities into their lesson plans to keep the students engaged.

Summer school programs are run similar to summer camps, but with an educational twist.

The social element of summer school is great for students. It can be hard for students to go months without seeing their friends, especially if they live far away or have family **obligations** during the summer.

When you are in summer school, you get to still spend time with your friends or make some new ones. Since being with friends is one of the best parts of summer anyway, summer school can end up being full of great memories for you.

Reality ✔

Research shows that socializing is an important part of childhood because it teaches skills that children will need throughout their lives.

Not every student goes to summer school in order to advance to the next grade. Some students might be there because they have nowhere else to go during the day.

A lot of parents work while their children are at school, so they may not always be able to find childcare or summer camp options that work for their schedules.

Summer school helps these families know their children are somewhere safe during the day. Parents can focus and feel less guilty because they know their kids are doing something fun and productive.

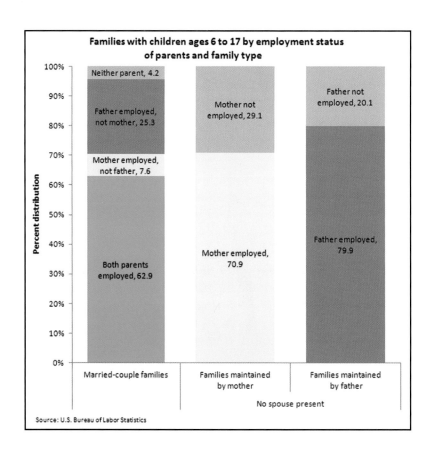

No matter what reason you have for attending summer school, it is important to have the option. So many students and their parents would be in a difficult position if they could not rely on summer school.

Summer school may not be a mandatory requirement, but it should definitely be an option for the people who need it.

Reality ✓

A national poll by researchers showed that the number of students who participate in summer programs has increased.

Summer School? No Way!

Summer is supposed to give students some time off from all of the busy and stressful things that go on during the school year. There is a good reason why it is called summer break. Students work so hard throughout the year, they deserve some time off to relax!

Summer school might be considered unfair because students get the chance to pass a class in a few weeks that others had to spend an entire year on.

Summer school has a **condensed**, or shorter, schedule because summer break is shorter than the school year.

Reality ✓

Different students learn at different paces. It can be more difficult for a slower learner to adapt to a faster pace of learning.

If some students have to spend months on a topic, why is it acceptable to let other students spend only a few days or weeks on it?

If it is possible to learn the material in half of the time, why wouldn't schools do it all year? This would allow some students to move through school faster or learn more while still having their summers free.

Summer school takes away the freedom that students need to relieve some of the pressure the school year places on them. Summer is a time for fun and discovery. You should be making new friends, going on vacation, or spending time with your family.

During the school year, everyone is often so busy with school, homework, and **extracurricular** activities that it can be hard to have quality time to spend together if you have to attend summer school.

If a family was planning to take a summer vacation, then they find out that one of their children has to stay in town for summer school, what do they do? Now they have to rearrange their entire trip, maybe even cancel it.

Summer school is not the only option to prevent students from being held back. Some schools offer after-school programs that take place throughout the school year for students who are in danger of failing.

Programs like this keep students on track during the school year. It also helps with time management.

Students who get this sort of ongoing help may be more likely to learn the subjects they are struggling with, because their after-school work builds on what they are currently learning.

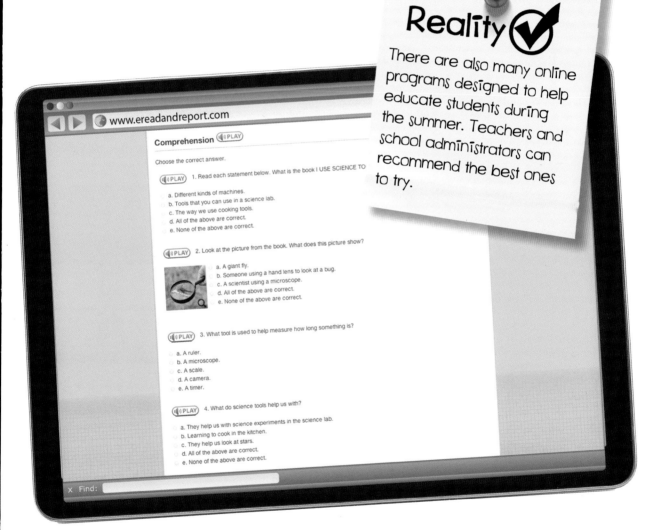

Reality ✓

There are also many online programs designed to help educate students during the summer. Teachers and school administrators can recommend the best ones to try.

If a student struggled with a subject when they had more time, what sense does it make to assume they will be able to learn it in a shorter time period?

No one knows if it really works. Education experts in the United States have admitted there is not a lot of data collected about the effectiveness of summer school.

Reality ✓

Education experts from the Education Commission of the States have said that more information about summer school in the U.S. is needed to determine if it is effective.

Education is **crucial** to a student's future, which is why there are so many studies and ongoing research projects to measure what works and does not work.

Without solid research to show how summer school works and what benefits it has on a student's education, it is difficult to measure the success of summer school programs.

Most students do not want to be there. It is harder to learn when your mind is distracted by other things. For students in summer school, there are a lot of things to think about.

This **distraction** can be difficult for students who have siblings, friends, or neighbors who do not have to attend summer school. It is hard to be in school while everyone else is having fun.

If you feel like you are missing out on a lot of fun, there is a good chance that you are not going to be focused on learning.

So if summer school is not helping you learn, then what is the point of being there?

Your Turn

After you have considered information from both sides of the issue, what do you think? Are you for or against summer school? Why do you feel that way? Can you think of new information that could add to your argument? Now it is your turn to **persuade** people with your point of view. Use data and personal experiences to write about your opinions.

A thoughtful discussion should let other people understand why you feel the way that you do about the issue.

Telling Your Side: Writing Opinion Pieces

- Tell your opinion first. Use phrases such as:
  - *I like _____.*
  - *I think_____.*
  - *_____ is the best _____.*
- Give multiple reasons to support your opinion. Use facts and relevant information instead of stating your feelings.
- Use the words *and*, *because*, and *also* to connect your opinion to your reasons.
- Clarify or explain your facts by using the phrases *for example* or *such as*.
- Compare your opinion to a different opinion. Then point out reasons that your opinion is better. You can use phrases *such as*:
- *Some people think_____, but I disagree because _____.*
- *_____ is better than _____ because _____.*
- Give examples of positive outcomes if the reader agrees with your opinion. For example, you can use the phrase, *If _____ then _____.*
- Use a personal story about your own experiences with your topic. For example, if you are writing about your opinion on after-school sports, you can write about your own experiences with after-school sports activities.
- Finish your opinion piece with a strong conclusion that highlights your strongest arguments. Restate your opinion so your reader remembers how you feel.

Glossary

condensed (kuhn-DENST): reduced in volume, area, length, or scope

continuity (kon-tuh-NEW-i-tee): a continuous or connected whole

crucial (KROO-shuhl): an extremely important decision or result

distraction (dih-STRAKT-shuhn): the act of drawing away or diverting the mind or attention

examine (ig-ZAM-in): to inspect or scrutinize carefully

extracurricular (ek-STRUH-kuh-rik-yuh-ler): outside the regular curriculum or program of courses

humiliating (hyoo-MIL-ee-a-ting): lowering the pride, self-respect, or dignity of a person

mastered (MAS-tuhrd): ability or power to use, control, or dispose of something

obligations (ahb-li-GAY-shuhns): a binding promise, contract, sense of duty, etc.

persuade (per-SWADE): to induce to believe by appealing to reason or understanding; convince

Index

Show What You Know

1. Some people may have never gone to summer school. How do you make an argument for something that you have never experienced?

2. Why is it important to learn how to write an opinion paper?

3. How do you form an opinion on a new subject?

4. What are some important parts of a strong argument and why are they important?

5. Do you think an opinion can change over time? Why or why not?

Websites to Visit

www.npr.org/sections/ed/2014/07/07/323659124/what-we-dont-know-about-summer-school

http://childparenting.about.com/od/schoollearning/a/is_summer_school_a_good_idea.htm

www.edutopia.org/blog/48-summer-websites-kids-teachers-keith-ferrell

About the Author

Erin Palmer is a writer and editor in Tampa, Florida, who lives with her three dogs: Bacon, Maybe, and Lucky. She thinks it is important to learn and have fun, no matter what season it is. Erin loves to read, travel, and spend time on the beach.

Meet The Author!
www.meetREMauthors.com

www.rourkeeducationalmedia.com

PHOTO CREDITS: Cover (top): ©TomPerkins; cover (bottom): ©Aleksander Kaczmarek; page 1: ©Steve Greer; page 3, 6, 22: ©Christopher Futcher; page 4 (top): ©Barcin; page 4 (bottom): ©jphotography; page 5: ©Tom Wang; page 6, 7,8,13,16,18, 23, 24: ©loops7; page 7: ©Yuri Arcurs; page 8: ©Neustockimages; page 9: ©Vikram Raghuvanshi; page 10: ©Westend61; page 11: ©Susan Chiang; page 13: ©lisafx; page 15: ©MilesStudio; page 16: ©Steve Debenport; page 17: ©Rodolfo Arguedos; page 18: ©princessdiaf; page 19: ©eurobanks; page 20-21: ©amriphoto; page 23: ©Atilla Altun; page 24-25, 27: ©Shanekato; page 26: ©Oko_SwanOmurphy; page 28: ©monkeybusiness images

Edited by: Keli Sipperley

Cover design and Interior design by: Rhea Magaro

Library of Congress PCN Data

Summer School, Yes or No / Erin Palmer
 (Seeing Both Sides)
  ISBN 978-1-68191-385-8 (hard cover)
  ISBN 978-1-68191-427-5 (soft cover)
  ISBN 978-1-68191-467-1 (e-Book)
Library of Congress Control Number: 2015951553

Also Available as:

Printed in the United States of America, North Mankato, Minnesota